BASKETBALL
BATS

ALSO IN THE *Gym Shorts* SERIES

Goof-Off Goalie

BASKETBALL BATS

Betty Hicks

Illustrated by Adam McCauley

ROARING BROOK PRESS
NEW YORK

Text copyright © 2008 by Betty Hicks
Illustrations copyright © 2008 by Adam McCauley

Published by Roaring Brook Press
Roaring Brook Press is a division of
Holtzbrinck Publishing Holdings Limited Partnership
175 Fifth Avenue, New York, New York 10010
www.roaringbrookpress.com

Library of Congress Cataloging-in-Publication Data
Hicks, Betty.
Basketball Bats / by Betty Hicks ; illustrated by Adam McCauley. — 1st ed.
p. cm. — (Gym shorts)
Summary: Henry and his basketball teammates, the Bats, take on the Tigers,
and Henry learns a lesson about working as a team.
ISBN-13: 978-1-59643-243-7   ISBN-10: 1-59643-243-8
[1. Basketball—Fiction. 2. Teamwork (Sports)—Fiction.]
I. McCauley, Adam, ill.   II. Title.
PZ7.H53155Bas 2008
[Fic]—dc22   2007019501

Roaring Brook Press books are available for special promotions and premiums.
For details, contact: Director of Special Markets, Holtzbrinck Publishers.

Book design by Jennifer Browne
Printed in the United States of America
First edition April 2008
2   4   6   8   10   9   7   5   3

For Eli

CONTENTS

BUG JUICE

Henry felt lucky. He had four friends.

Exactly enough to make a basketball team.

To Henry, playing sports was better than triple-scoop ice cream. Better than the circus coming to town. Better than anything.

Henry dribbled the ball just inside the chalk line he'd drawn across his driveway. It marked the boundary of his backyard basketball court.

He did a spin move and drove for the basket. A layup is too easy, thought Henry. Instead, he pulled up short. He aimed and threw up a mid-range jump shot. *Swish!*

"I could squash you like a bug," snarled a gruff voice.

"Huh?" Henry stared at the boy at the top of his driveway. He had spiky hair. His body slouched to one side.

"Me and my friends," said Tough Guy. "The Tigers.
We can beat anybody."

"Yeah?" said Henry.

"Well, my friends are good, too."

"I doubt it," sneered Tough Guy.

I'd like to squash *him* like a bug, thought Henry.

But he didn't say it out loud. Instead, he said, "We challenge you. Tomorrow. Right here—three o'clock."

"Your funeral," said Tough Guy.

GROUP GROWL

The next day, Henry's friends formed a circle around him: Goose, Rocky, Rita, and Jazz.

Rocky's bulldog, Chops, squeezed himself into the space between their legs.

"Anybody here afraid of Tigers?" asked Henry.

Jazz's bright eyes danced with excitement. "Are you kidding?"

Rocky shrugged. "Not me."

Goose grinned his famous goofball grin.

Rita twirled on one toe like a ballet dancer. "We are the champions!" she sang.

Yes! thought Henry.

He had four good friends. They all lived on the same street. *And*, they were a team.

"Let's practice before Tough Guy and the Tigers show up," said Henry. He tossed the ball to Rocky.

Rocky dribbled it—one, two, three times. He heaved
the ball into the air.

Swish! The ball dropped through the net as if it
had eyes. Three points! Rocky was deadly from three-
point land.

Henry raced under the net and scooped it up.

Jazz zipped in. Just like she always did—quicker
than a blink. And stole the ball from Henry.

She passed it off to Goose, who raced toward the

basket. His long arm guided the ball straight up and in.

Goose grinned his goofball grin again. He pumped his arm and shouted, "Yes!"

"We . . . are . . . good!" sang Rita, twirling again.

Henry threw one fist into the air. "We can beat anybody!"

Then they heard it—a *grrrr* sound. They turned.

Tough Guy and his team were grinding out group growls at the top of Henry's driveway.

Henry couldn't believe it. Neither could Chops. Rocky's dog cocked his head.

Tough Guy and each of his friends wore T-shirts with tigers on them. Big, mean, yellow tigers. With lots of teeth.

Henry's friends didn't have fancy T-shirts.

They didn't even have a team name.

Would the Tigers squash him like a bug?

"Who gets the ball first?" asked the only girl Tiger.

"We can have a jump ball," suggested Henry. "I'll toss it up."

"No way," said Tough Guy.

Henry shrugged. "Okay. *You* toss it up."

"Wrong again," said Tough Guy. "*I'll* jump." He flipped the ball to Girl Tiger. "She'll toss it up."

You are a jerk, thought Henry.

He checked out the rest of the Tiger team.

One Tiger wore new sneakers. One of those cool brands that cost a lot.

Another Tiger had crazy orange hair. "Hey, Carrot," called Fancy Shoe Boy.

Carrot? All his life Henry had wanted a nickname. But *Carrot?* Whoa! That name stunk. Even if the kid's hair was the color of a crayon.

The fifth Tiger was a huge kid with a squishy, moon face. Not tall. Just big. As if he ate a donut every five minutes.

Henry wondered if Big Kid had a nickname. He hoped it wasn't anything mean.

Girl Tiger held the basketball straight out with one hand. Ready to toss it up.

Tough Guy crouched. Ready to jump.

Goose stood on Girl Tiger's other side.

She tossed the ball into the air.

Only she didn't throw it straight up. She threw it slanted, toward Tough Guy. He grabbed the ball and raced for the basket.

"Not fair!" Henry shouted.

Girl Tiger smiled.

This team has two jerks, thought Henry.

NO FAIR, NO FOUL

Henry's team was playing Tough Guy's.

The Tigers had cheated on the opening ball toss. No time to worry about it.

Goose scrambled back on defense. Tough Guy streaked in for a layup.

Goose blocked his shot. He swatted it so hard it flew straight into Henry's mother's tulips.

Henry wanted to scream, *in your face!* at the Tigers. But he didn't want to be a bad sport.

The ball bounced once. Squashed six flowers. And landed in the birdbath. *Splash!*

Jazz scooped the ball out of the water. She dried it on her shorts. Then she threw it to Henry.

Henry saw Rocky standing in his favorite spot. A mile from the basket. So far out, the Tigers didn't guard him.

Henry passed Rocky the ball. He caught it and dribbled three times. Rocky always dribbled three times. Then he heaved a three-point shot into the air.

Swish.

The Tigers all growled again. They crowded together. They slapped a group high five. And they *growled.*

Then Fancy Shoe Boy threw the ball in. Just like a normal person. As if he hadn't been making jungle noises five seconds ago.

Carrot Hair caught it.

That's when Jazz zipped in. Just like she always did. She stole the ball right out of his hands.

"She fouled him!" cried Shoe Boy.

"Did not," said Jazz. "I never touched him!"

Carrot Hair's face told the truth. It flushed red.

Well, thought Henry. *One* Tiger plays fair.

Jazz tossed the ball to Henry. He sprinted for the basket. He planned to pull up short and shoot his favorite jump shot.

Instead, he spotted Rita. With her frizzy dark red hair. She was wide open under the basket.

He bounced a pass around Big Kid.

Big Kid turned. Too slow. Too late. "*Nooo,*" he moaned. Henry almost felt sorry for him.

Rita put it up and into the hoop. She twirled and floated like a dancer in her ruffly clothes. Rita dressed girly, but she was tougher than sharks' teeth.

"The score's five to nothing," said Goose, quietly. But his hands were so happy, they twitched.

Henry guessed Goose was trying to be a good sport, too.

The Tigers didn't growl. They just stomped to the back of the court and started over.

They made a few shots, but Henry and his friends killed them. Thirty-six to twenty.

"We want a rematch," whined Shoe Boy.

"Sure," said Henry.

Rita, Jazz, Rocky, and Goose all nodded.

"How about two out of three?" asked Rocky.

"Done," barked Tough Guy. "Only, next time, it has to be fair."

Henry balled up his fists. "This was fair!" he snapped. Being a good sport was getting harder.

"You call this fake court *fair*?" sneered Tough Guy. "You play on it every day. We've *never* played here. Besides—look at it!"

He waved his hand around. As if he were pointing at a driveway covered with roadkill. "The basket's not even the right height."

"It is, too!" Henry jammed his fists on his hips and glared.

"Next game's on *our* turf," said Tough Guy. He jerked his thumb at his puffed-out chest.

"Fine." Henry spit out the word. Before he had time to think.

Then, he stopped.

Their turf?

Where *was* Tiger turf?

BECOMING A BAT

"Can you believe them?" said Henry. "Tigers! Ha!"

"Jerks," said Goose.

"Where *is* Tiger turf?" asked Rita.

"India," answered Jazz. "Tigers live in India."

Henry nodded. Jazz knew stuff.

"We need a name, too," said Rocky. He sat in the driveway, fishing a rock out of his shoe.

"Totally," agreed Rita. "We'll name ourselves—"

"—after the street we live on," suggested Jazz. "Rockford." She clapped her hands. "The Rockford Rockets!"

Rita pumped her arms. She did a wiggly dance with her hips. "We are the Rock-ets—the Rockford Rock-ets."

"I like rockets," said Goose. He reached into his shirt pocket and pulled out a Tootsie Pop.

It looked grape flavored. But it had too much fuzz on it to tell for sure. He wiped it on his sleeve and slid it into his mouth.

"*Eeew,*" said Rita.

"We'll need T-shirts," said Rocky. He stuffed his foot back into his sneaker.

"Yeah!" Henry threw up his arms. "With a giant rocket on them, blasting into space."

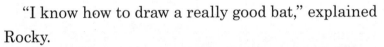

"*Or a bat,*" said Rocky.

"A bat?" they all asked together.

"I know how to draw a really good bat," explained Rocky.

Goose curled his tongue out to show everyone that it was purple. "Food dye," he said. Then he licked the Tootsie Pop and asked, "A *baseball* bat?"

Rocky picked up the piece of chalk Henry had used to mark the basketball court.

"*Not* a baseball bat," he said. His voice sounded more serious than a math test. "A vampire bat."

Rocky stretched flat on his stomach in the middle of Henry's driveway. Chops trotted over and licked his nose.

Everyone, even Chops, watched Rocky draw. Slowly, a very awesome bat, with tiny terrible teeth, appeared on the concrete.

"Coooool," they all whispered in one long breath.

"Yeah . . . but, guys," Henry said, "where's our next game? *Their* turf. Remember? I'm guessing it's somewhere a lot closer than India."

"Who hares," said Goose. His cheek bulged full of Tootsie Pop again.

"What?" asked Henry.

Goose pulled out the lollipop. "Who cares?" he repeated. "So long as we get T-shirts."

"Yeah," said Henry. "Who cares?"

But he knew exactly who cared.

He did.

THE SLAM-DUNK KID

Two mornings later, Henry woke up. He still didn't know where Tiger turf was.

But he decided not to worry. As long as he could play ball, he'd be happy.

After all, Henry loved sports. His room was filled with trophies. Baseball, basketball, tennis, swimming. You name it. He had *three* trophies for soccer.

Well . . . the basketball trophy was for most improved in PE. He hadn't actually played on a *real* team. At

Henry's school, you had to be in fifth grade to be on the basketball team.

One more year, thought Henry.

Only now, he *was* on a team. With a name. The Bats.

Henry heard ringing. The phone. Somewhere under his bed. How'd it get there? he wondered. He fumbled until he found it.

"Guess what?" said Jazz's voice.

"What?" asked Henry.

"A Tiger called me. I know where their turf is."

"Where?"

"The YWCA."

"The new one?"

"Yeah."

"The really big brand-new one?"

"Yeah. One of their mothers coaches there. The court's free for thirty minutes. She signed us up."

"When."

"Today."

"*Today*! *Yes*!" Henry cheered. Then he remembered. "We don't have T-shirts." He slumped. "Mom

says I have to pay for mine." He sagged lower. "I'm broke."

"Well," said Jazz. "If we win two games, my dad said he'll buy shirts for everyone."

"No kidding!" Henry bolted straight up. "Thanks, Jazz."

He jumped out of bed. He threw on the first clothes he stepped on.

In the bathroom, he squeezed blue toothpaste onto his toothbrush. *If we can beat the Tigers one more time, we get T-shirts.*

Henry thought it would be so cool to have a bat T-shirt. One designed by Rocky. One that no one else on the planet owned. Just Henry and his four best friends.

Even better, if they beat the Tigers one more time, Tough Guy would know that he wasn't. Tough.

Henry scrubbed his teeth as if he were trying to

wipe the Tigers off the face of the earth.

He stared in the mirror. He had worked up major suds. As a matter of fact, he looked rabid. Crazy. Foaming at the mouth—like a mad dog.

Mad Dog Henry, he thought, and wished, for the millionth time, that he had a nickname.

Everybody has a nickname, he thought, spitting into the sink. Rocky's named after the movie boxer who never gave up. Jazz's real name is Jasmine.

Rita is short for Margarita. And Goose's name is Brian.

He is really *not* a Brian.

Then there's me. He pitched his voice low and boomed at the mirror. "*Heeenry!*" He tried to make it sound manly.

It didn't.

The name was so boring. Worse, there was no way to shorten it. Except to Hen.

"*Cluck, buck, buck, cluck!*" Henry tucked his hands under his armpits. He flapped his arms like a chicken.

He sloshed water inside his mouth. He aimed it at a blue glob of toothpaste on the left side of the sink. *Splat*! He nailed it!

Hotshot Henry.

He spit the next mouthful straight down the drain. "*Sploosh*!"

The Slam-dunk Kid!

Could being a Bat earn him a nickname? Definitely.

Could it earn him a nickname *today*? He'd find out.

TIGER TURF

Henry stepped into the huge YWCA gym with his team. He felt tiny. Like a bug.

He looked up. It was a mile to the rafters.

He looked down. The floor was so shiny he could see his face. The squeaky-clean newness smelled like rubber.

Henry felt three things at once.

1. Excited.

He was about to play basketball on an awesome new court.

2. Nervous.

He was about to play basketball on an awesome new court.

3. Fear.

They might not get T-shirts.

Worse. They might not beat Tough Guy.

Henry had played on enough teams to know—sometimes the bad guy comes in first.

Then he spotted Tough Guy. Strutting around as if he were the boss of everything. Ordering his team to shoot layups. Then free throws. "*Now* we'll get to play fair," he boasted.

Henry doubted it. He wondered who the older kid was—the one wearing a Tiger T-shirt. He was shooting free throws with the other Tigers.

Rita pointed at him. "Who's he?"

No one answered.

Rita poked Tough Guy on the arm and repeated. "Who's he?"

Tough Guy rubbed his arm and said, "Huh?" As if he couldn't see the six-foot-tall kid. The one who looked like a teenager and was nailing a free throw every four seconds.

"Oh," said Tough Guy. "That's my cousin." He shrugged a no-big-deal shrug and added, "He's subbing on our team today."

Subbing? thought Henry. He looked around the huge gym. Big Kid from the first game was nowhere in

sight. Teen Boy was subbing for Big Kid?

"Are you kidding me?" yelped Henry. "How old is that guy?"

"Eleven," said Tough Guy. He said it so fast, Henry knew it was a lie.

"Eleven!" exclaimed Henry. "How about thirteen!"

"Or fourteen," said Rita.

Henry looked to Carrot Hair for help. He was honest. Wasn't he?

But Carrot was quietly studying his toes. His face flushed brighter than his hair.

"My cousin," said Tough Guy, "is in fifth grade."

"Yeah," sneered Goose. "And I'm Peter Pan."

"Okay, kids!" A woman in pink-and-gray warm-ups clapped her hands. "We only have this court for thirty minutes."

"Who's *that!*" Henry blurted.

"My mother," said Tough Guy. "She's our referee."

Henry whirled around. *What!* He turned to his friends. This was not fair!

The Bats looked dazed. They stared from Tough Guy's mother—the referee!—to his teenage cousin—the sub! He was still drilling free throws.

He had a fuzzy dark shadow on his upper lip. He needed to shave!

We are doomed, thought Henry.

7

HOT DOG

How do I bail out of this stupid, really, really not fair game? Henry wondered.

He could say, *I have homework to do.* Or, *I don't want to miss my trip to the dentist.* Maybe he could say, *My house is on fire.*

"Jump ball!" cried Tough Guy's mom. "I need a Bat over here."

Goose clenched his fists. He walked over to jump against Teen Boy.

Okay, thought Henry. If Goose can do this, so can I.

The Bats surrounded the jump-ball circle. Jazz crouched low.

"Think T-shirts," said Rocky.

"Think beating stupid cheaters," grumbled Henry.

"Just think," said Rita.

Teen Boy towered over Goose. He didn't even have to jump. He just reached up and swatted the ball to a waiting teammate.

At least Tough Guy's mother tossed it straight. Maybe she'd be fair.

The Tigers passed it back to Teen Boy. He went in for an easy layup. Henry wouldn't have been surprised to see him dunk it.

Two to nothing—Tigers.

Jazz tossed the ball in to Henry, who dribbled toward half-court. He saw Rocky in his spot. He passed him the ball.

But Girl Tiger and Teen Boy double-teamed Rocky before he could dribble all three times.

They stole the ball.

Two more Tiger points.

Next time, Henry made sure he got the ball to Jazz. She could out-quick anybody.

Not this time. Teen Boy blocked her shot. Straight

into the last row of the bleachers. Just like he was
swatting a fly.

Goose, thought Henry. Get the ball to Goose.
Where's Goose?

Henry spotted him—at the wrong end of the court.
Leaning over. Grasping his gym shorts. Panting.

Goose never ran full court. None of the Bats did.

Tough Guy made an easy layup.

Six to nothing.

The Bats formed a quick huddle in the middle of
the court.

"Next time," grumbled Jazz. "Let's use *my* cousin. He plays in the NBA."

"Really?" asked Rocky.

"No." Jazz laughed. "But maybe my mother could ref."

"Yeah," said Goose. "If they can cheat, why shouldn't we?"

Henry stayed silent, but he was thinking, *No one has a clue. I guess it's up to me.*

Next play, he ignored Rita. Even though she was wide open under the basket. Instead, Henry drove straight for the hoop.

Teen Boy was waiting. The face-that-needed-a-shave loomed over Henry like something out of a horror movie.

Henry gulped. He shut his eyes. He fired up a panic shot. It missed the whole basket.

"Air ball!" jeered Tough Guy.

Henry wanted to kill him. Instead, he fouled him.

Tough Guy stood at the foul line. Showing off his biceps. He sank two free throws.

Eight to zip.

"Hey, Hot Dog," Goose wheezed to Henry. "You're not a one-man team, you know."

Hot Dog! Henry's face flushed red. His ears burned. Henry couldn't believe Goose had called him that.

Man! He'd always wanted a nickname. But not *that* one.

He snatched the ball and dribbled downcourt. Faster than anyone.

Except Teen Boy.

When Henry threw up his favorite jump shot, Teen Boy hacked his elbow. Pain screamed up his arm.

32

Henry sucked in air. His shot dropped through the net anyway.

Yes! Eight to two.

And, Henry had a foul shot coming. A chance for a three-point play!

Except, the ref didn't call the foul. She hadn't seen it. She was too busy chugging Gatorade out of a squeeze bottle.

The Bats lost. Forty to nineteen. Fifteen of the Bats' points had come from Henry.

Henry slunk off the court with his teammates. He could barely breathe. He needed air. He needed water.

He knew they'd never get T-shirts. It wasn't fair. Cheaters shouldn't win.

"Hey, Hot Dog," said Rita, panting. "You could've passed the ball—"

Henry stared at Rita. He looked at the rest of the Bats.

They stared back. His friends. All of them. Angry.

They blamed him? Hadn't he scored almost all their points?

Geez. *Nothing* was fair.

WAFFLE MAGIC

Henry sat at breakfast with his elbow on the table. He propped his head up with one hand. With the other hand, he poured maple syrup over his homemade waffle.

Henry loved waffles. He *used* to love sports. Now he wasn't sure.

Maybe the Bats *should* cheat. But how? Henry didn't have any cousins older than seven.

"Nothing's fair," he groaned.

Click-tick, click-tick-tick-tick. Henry's mother typed on her laptop at the same table with Henry. Dad set two waffles down beside her computer.

He poured more batter into the steaming-hot waffle iron. Henry's kitchen smelled better than a bakery.

"Is anybody listening?" said Henry. He stabbed a chunk of waffle as if it were Tough Guy.

"Sorry, honey," answered Mom. "Give me five minutes. I have *got* to finish this before I go to work."

"All right," said Dad. "I'm listening. What's not
fair?"

"Cheaters win," said Henry.

Dad nodded. "Sometimes they do, but not—"

"And my friends think I'm selfish," said Henry. He
stuffed the whole wad of waffle into his mouth. Syrup
dripped down his chin.

"Really?" Dad raised his eyebrows.

"They called me *Hot Dog Henry.*"

"Wipe your chin, son."

"They think I'm a ball hog," said Henry. He jammed more waffle into his mouth. "But, Dad! I had to do something! We were getting—"

"Chew with your mouth closed," said Dad. "You can't choose what people call you."

"Like we could beat those guys if I passed the ball! Yeah, right."

Henry reached across the table and speared one of his mom's waffles. He slapped it onto his own plate.

Click-tick-click-tick. Click-click-click.

"I'm a team player!" Henry shouted.

"You are," Dad agreed.

"Have you ever seen me hog the ball?"

"No, son."

"Or be selfish?"

"Well, you did just steal your mother's waffle."

"Dad! I'm serious."

"Me, too. Give your mother back her waffle."

Henry handed back the stolen waffle.

Mom looked up from her computer. "You are *my* team player," she said. She reached over and squeezed Henry's hand.

Henry stared at his empty plate. "It's still not fair."

"I'm cooking another batch," said Dad.

"No," said Henry. "I meant it's not fair that my friends think I hog the ball."

"And *I* meant that waffles can help," said Dad. "Keep being you. Eat waffles. Have syrup. Play ball. They'll come around."

"Your father's right," said Mom.

Dad handed Henry a fresh stack of hot waffles.

"Thanks," said Henry. But he was thinking, *Parents are weird.*

He poured more syrup onto his plate. It streamed over the waffles, filling each little square.

It trickled over, covering the plate around them. Henry kept pouring.

Around and around and around.

That's when it hit him! The answer.

Henry knew how to change his friends' minds. *And* beat the stupid Tigers.

THE BAT DRESS

The first thing Henry did was finish his waffles. They had so much syrup on them, it made his teeth hurt.

It was worth it.

The second thing he did was ask Dad for one of his white T-shirts.

"Sure. Try my dresser. Under my socks. You should find some old ones."

Henry poked around and found two. One had a rip at the bottom. The other had yellow armpits. Henry chose the ripped one.

Next he grabbed a black ink marker and a red one. He hurried outside. *Yes!* Rocky's bat drawing still covered the driveway.

Henry copied it onto the front of his dad's old shirt. His bat wasn't as good as Rocky's, but it was the best he could do.

He uncapped the red marker and added blood drops to the bat's teeth. He held it up.

Nice.

Then he telephoned Jazz.

"Yeah?" She didn't sound happy to hear from him.

"We can beat the Tigers," said Henry.

"Yeah?" She sounded doubtful. "How?"

"I'll explain later. Didn't one of them call you? Did you keep their number?"

"Yeah," said Jazz.

"Great," said Henry. "I need you to call it. Ask if they'll meet us on a neutral court. At the park. Three thirty."

Henry waited. Silence.

Had the phone gone dead?

"Jazz," he pleaded, "I have a plan that will work. Trust me."

"Trust you?"

"Yes. Please. Come on. I'm not a hot dog. You know me. I'm doing this for our team. We can win. I swear. . . ."

"Okay."

"Thanks, Jazz!"

Henry hung up. Then he called Rocky, Goose, and Rita. He asked them to be at the park earlier than the Tigers. At three fifteen. They said they'd be there.

Jazz called back. The Tigers would come.

Yes!

Henry arrived at the park before anyone. He wiped his sweaty palms on his shirt. Why did they get so drippy when he was nervous?

He rubbed his face and worried. Was his idea stupid?

His fingers kept sticking to his chin. Oh, yeah. Syrup.

Rita, Goose, Rocky, and Jazz arrived together.

Rocky's dog, Chops, jumped against Henry's leg. He licked his knee.

At least somebody still likes me, thought Henry.

"Yo, Hot Dog. What's up?" said Goose.

Henry moaned. "Don't call me that. Please?"

"How about Ball Hog?" teased Rita.

Henry clenched his fists. "I didn't . . . Look . . . I was just trying—" He unclenched his fists. He patted Chops. "Never mind. Just listen. Okay?"

They stared. Waiting.

"As long as the Tigers have Teen Boy—*and* lie about his age—we're dead. Right?"

"Right."

"Unless we outsmart them. Right?"

Silence.

"Look. We don't play their whole team. We challenge *one* of them. To a game of Around the World. Their best player against our best player. No refs. No rules. Whoever makes the most shots from ten spots around the basket."

Henry waited. "I'm a genius, right?"

The Bats looked at each other. As if they didn't know what to think.

Henry held up his dad's torn T-shirt. "Our player wears this!"

"That?" said Rita. "*Eeew.*"

"You're wearing *that*?" asked Goose.

"Me?" said Henry. "No. Rocky is."

More silence.

Then, "Yes!" "Rocky!" "Brilliant!"

Rocky bit his lower lip. He tried not to grin.

Henry tossed him the shirt. The rest of the Bats chanted, "Rocky, Rocky! You the man!"

42

Rocky pulled the shirt over his head. It swallowed him like a circus tent.

"Oops," said Henry.

Rocky looked down, trying to find his feet. "What?"

Chops cocked his head.

"Nothing," said Henry. "You look great."

"Who's the kid in the bat dress?" asked Tough Guy.

YOU THE MAN!

"Am I wearing a dress?" Rocky whispered.

"Don't worry," said Rita. She twisted, pulled, and tucked the fabric of the too-big T-shirt. Then she stepped back. "Ta-da!"

It did look better.

"So," said Tough Guy. "What's the plan?"

"Who's our ref?" asked Shoe Boy.

"That bat looks stupid," said Girl Tiger.

"There is no ref," explained Henry. "The Bats challenge the Tigers—" Henry paused. In his brain he heard a drumroll "—to one game of Around the World. You pick your best shooter. We pick ours. Winner breaks the tie."

And—Henry crossed his fingers—*good guys win. Cheaters lose. Plus, we get T-shirts.*

Tough Guy laughed. "The Bats are batty."

"Bonkers," said Girl Tiger.

Shoe Boy pointed to Teen Boy. "We pick him."

"Well, duh," Goose mumbled.

"We pick Rocky," said Jazz.

The Tigers laughed.

"Your best shooter wears a dress," hissed Tough Guy.

Rocky swung out his arms. He bent forward and down. All Rita's tucks popped loose. He curtsied. "I eat Tigers for lunch," he said.

Henry laughed. For a short kid, Rocky was huge.

Rita twisted and re-tucked Rocky's shirt.

Henry drew a huge half circle, way out from the basket. He marked ten places on it with *X*s. "Fair?" he asked.

"Fair," said the Tigers. Then they *grrred* their group growl.

Did they know *how stupid they sounded?*

Rocky tied Chops's leash to a bush. He rubbed his ears for luck. Then he stepped up to the first spot. Henry handed him the ball.

Rocky dribbled three times. But the T-shirt sleeves got in his way. He heaved the ball up anyway.

Whoosh.

"Air ball!" chanted the Tigers

Nooo, Henry groaned inside.

Rocky jerked at his shirt. Rita's fix had come undone again. Rocky was back to wearing a circus tent.

Teen Boy pushed Rocky aside. He stood on the *X* and fired up a high, arcing shot. *Swish.*

Tigers 1. Bats 0.

"Take the shirt off," said Henry.

"No." Rocky waved him away. "I'm fine."

He stepped up to the second mark. Three dribbles. One shot. *Swish.*

Yes!

Teen Boy shrugged and made the same shot. "In your face, Rocky."

Tigers 2. Bats 1.

Rocky and Teen Boy traded shots at five more spots before Teen Boy finally missed one. That tied the score. 6 to 6.

Rocky fired up a shot from X number eight. It hit the backboard and bounced in. Teen Boy's shot rimmed the basket. It circled twice and fell through.

7 to 7.

Rocky's next shot came in flat and bounced up off the rim.

Goose groaned. Jazz gasped.

The ball fell back through the net. A miracle.

Teen Boy stepped up to spot number nine. He looked stiff. Tense. He rolled his shoulders.

He's going to miss it, thought Henry.

Teen Boy dribbled once and fired up his shot. It dropped straight through the net.

Henry couldn't believe it.

Game tied. 8 to 8. Only one *X* left.

Rocky seemed tired. Teen Boy looked nervous.

"Rocky, Rocky. You the man!" cheered the Bats.

"Kill him!" shouted the Tigers.

Rocky took a slow, deep breath. At least it looked like he did. He was so covered up with T-shirt, it was hard to tell. He dribbled three times. His shot arced high. Orange ball against blue sky. The Bats froze.

Swish.

Rita shrieked.

"Nothing but net," howled Goose.

"Shut up," growled the Tigers.

The Bats fell silent.

"Move," Teen Boy snarled at Rocky. He stepped onto the last X.

This was it.

The Bats crossed their fingers.

The Tigers held their breath.

Teen Boy twirled the ball on one finger.

Now *that's* a hot dog! thought Henry.

Teen Boy planted his feet, bent his knees, and shot

the ball. High. Soaring. Straight. Almost.

Clang! It hit the rim and bounced left.

Bats win! *9 to 8*!

The Bats swarmed Rocky. Goose lifted him onto his shoulders.

They all chanted, "Rocky! Rocky! You the man!"

Chops ran around in circles.

The Tigers slunk quietly away.

THIRD PLACE

Henry and his friends sat in the grass by the lake at the park. They elbowed each other and laughed. Chops took turns licking everybody.

Henry pounded Rocky on the back. "You were amazing."

"Thanks," said Rocky. He gave Henry a push. "It was your idea."

"You were both brilliant," said Goose.

Henry beamed. They were a team. They'd won. They'd played fair. And he, Henry, had figured out how.

"So," Henry asked, "no more Hot Dog?"

"Definitely not," said Rita.

"Yeah, Henry," added Jazz. "We're sorry."

"Well," said Goose, grinning like a goofball. "I kind of like it. Hot Dog Henry." He stuck a Tootsie Pop in his mouth. "It sounds good."

"No, it doesn't," said Henry.

"You always wanted a nickname," said Goose.

"Not that one."

"You don't get to choose," said Goose.

Man, thought Henry, he sounds like Dad.

A mother goose waddled by. Six small goslings hurried to catch up.

Henry and his friends smiled at the chorus of nervous baby quacks.

Rocky held Chops by his collar.

The geese slipped into the water and swam away from the shore.

Everyone had to be thinking the same thing Henry was thinking. Finally, Rocky said it. "Um, Goose. How come you're called Goose?"

"Who knows?" Goose shrugged. "Dad dreamed it up when I was little. Maybe it rhymed with loose."

"Maybe you had a long neck."

"Maybe you honked."

"Maybe you ate birdseed."

"Maybe you want a punch in the gut," said Goose.

"It's a great nickname," said Henry. "It fits you. But *Hot Dog*. It's so . . . so . . . mean."

"It's a wiener," said Rocky.

"How about Henry Hero?" said Jazz.

Rita and Goose stuck fingers down their own throats and gagged.

"How about just Henry?" asked Henry.

"It's boring," said Goose.

"No, it's not," said Henry.

"Look!" Jazz cried. "There's Dad." She leaped up and pointed to a silver van pulling into the parking lot.

The driver honked and shouted, "Who won?"

"We did!" screamed the Bats. They all pumped their fists into the air.

Jazz's dad waved something white and flappy in the air.

"Is that—?" Henry was afraid to ask.

"Yep," said Jazz, grinning. Her bright eyes sparkled.

"How'd he know?"

"He got Rocky to draw the bat—on paper. Then he

ordered five shirts. Right away. He *knew* we could do it."

Jazz's dad was swinging T-shirts in the air as if they were lassos. "Come and get them!"

Henry and his friends jumped up and raced for the van. Chops took the lead.

"Last one there's a Tiger!" shouted Rocky.

"*First* one there's a Hot Dog," said Goose.

That sounded fair to Henry.

He came in third. He made sure of it.

Happy Valley School
3855 Happy Valley Road
Lafayette, CA 94549